The Snow Party

Beatrice Schenk de Regniers

The Snow

Party

illustrated by Bernice Myers

Lothrop, Lee & Shepard Books   New York

First Edition   1 2 3 4 5 6 7 8 9 10

Library of Congress Cataloging in Publication Data
De Regniers, Beatrice Schenk. The snow party / by Beatrice de Regniers: illustrated by Bernice Myers.
p.   cm.   Summary: On a snowy, windy night at a Dakota farm, a lonely woman wishes for company,
music, and a party—and suddenly all her wishes start to come true.   ISBN 0-688-08570-9.
ISBN 0-688-08571-7 (lib. bdg.)   [1. Parties—Fiction. 2. Snow—Fiction.]   I. Myers, Bernice, ill.
II. Title.   PZ7.D4417Sn   1989   [E]—dc19
88-13332 CIP AC

For Helen Wolff,
and for Dan

There was this woman, and there was this man, and they lived in a little old farmhouse way out in Dakota.

And the woman said, "I'm mighty lonely here with just you and the chickens for company. I'd like to give me a party and have plenty of folks in."

And the man said, "What's the matter with you, woman? Are you daft? We don't know a soul to invite to a party.

"And if we did know a soul, who would come to a party through all this wind and snow?"

The woman looked out the window. She could see that outside it was snowing and snowing, and she could hear the wind blowing.

She said, "I'd bake me a cake and put candles on it, and I'd hire me a fiddler to fiddle a tune, and there would be feasting and dancing and merrymaking. There would be high jinks and low jinks. It would be a fine party, I can tell you."

"Woman, are you daft?" said the farmer. "Even if we knew a soul to invite to a party, and even if they came through the wind and the snow, we don't have a crust nor a crumb of cake nor a thimbleful of flour in the house to bake one."

Outside, it was snowing and snowing, and the wind was blowing.

Inside, the woman turned on all the lights so the house wouldn't look so lonely. She turned on the radio so the house wouldn't sound so lonely.

Someone on the radio was advertising the K-M Bakery. He was saying, "The next time you have a party, order K-M's simply heavenly chocolate fudge cake. And remember, the K-M Bakery delivers its delicious cakes, bread, pies, cupcakes, cinnamon rolls, and buns right to your door. So...

When you hear that
knock-knock
knock-knock-knock
answer the door as fast as you can,
'cause
knock-knock
knock-knock-knock
means
here comes the K-M man!"

"Chocolate cake," the woman sighed. "Cinnamon rolls, buns…"

Then all of a sudden the wind blew hard and harder, and it blew down the electric lines.

The radio went off and the lights went out, and it was dark in the little house.

So the woman lit candles. She had a lot of candles, and she lit them all and put them on the table.

The table looked like a big birthday cake, it had so many candles all around it.

"I wish it were a cake," said the woman. "I wish the table were a big cake and we were having a party."

"Hush, woman," said the man. "Wishes won't wash dishes, and wishes won't stop the wind from blowing or the snow from snowing." And he put on his high galoshes and his overcoat, and his hat and his earmuffs and his mittens.

"Where are you going in all this snow and wind?" asked the woman.

"We have three hundred baby chicks in the barn, and I'm going to bring them into the house to keep them warm. Three hundred chirping chicks will be company enough."

"Well, bring in the chicks," said the woman, "but that's not the company I'm wishing for."

The man went out the back door to the barn with the snow snowing and the wind blowing.

Listen!

There is a knock at the front door—*knock-knock*!

The woman hurries to the door. "Who could be knocking at our door," she says, "on a night like this with the snow snowing and the wind blowing?"

She opens the door, and in comes a great blast of wind and snow, and there stands a tall man saying, "My car is stuck in the snow with a carload of people. Would you be good enough to let us come in out of the snow and the wind until the snowplow comes to clear the road?"

"Come in, come in," says the woman. "Bring your carload of people, and welcome!" She scoops up a pot of snow and puts it on the stove to boil to make a pot of hot tea.

The tall man goes to his car and brings back his wife and her mother and his three brothers-in-law. His wife is carrying a tiny baby wrapped in a blanket.

The farmer is bringing in a box of chirping chicks. He says, "Welcome, welcome. Make yourselves at home. My woman was wishing for company." Then he picks up a basket and goes out the back door again to bring in some more baby chicks.

Listen!

There is a knock at the front door—*knock-knock!*

The woman hurries to the door. There in the wind and the snow stand a man and his wife and their twin boys and another man and a big hunting dog.

Their car is stuck in the snow, and they are waiting for the snowplow to come through and clear the road.

"Come in, come in," says the woman, "and welcome! There's plenty of hot tea to drink, though there's not a crust nor a crumb of cake or bread in the house to eat with it."

Then the farmer comes in with a basket of chirping chicks. Now there are eleven grown-ups and one baby and two little boys and a big hunting dog in the house.

"Welcome, welcome," says the farmer. "My woman was wishing for company, and now she has it." And once again he goes out the back door and into the wind and snow to bring in more baby chicks.

Outside, the snow is snowing and the wind is blowing, and the strangers are glad to be inside.

But listen!

Someone is knocking at the front door—*knock-knock*!

The woman hurries to the door, and there are three carloads of people. Their cars are stuck in the snow, and they must wait for the snowplow to come through and clear the road.

"Come in, come in," says the woman, "and welcome!"

So now when the farmer comes in the back door with a box of chirping baby chicks, he counts twenty-seven grown-ups, five children, three babies, two dogs, and a parakeet.

"Welcome, welcome," says the farmer. "My woman was wishing for company, and now she has it."

But listen!

Someone is knocking at the front door—*knock-knock*!

The woman hurries to the door, and the farmer comes with her.

There is only one man standing at the door in the wind and the snow. He says, "The snow is snowing and the wind is blowing, and my bus is stuck in the snow. May I wait inside till the snowplow comes?"

"Come in, come in," says the woman, "and welcome!"

So the bus driver goes to the bus and comes back with forty-two grown-ups, seven children, two babies, three dogs, a canary, and a little pet skunk.

"Welcome, welcome," says the man. "My woman was wishing for company, and now she has it."

"If only," says the woman, "if only there were a crust or a crumb of cake or bread in the house."

Listen!

Someone is knocking at the front door—*knock-knock*! And someone is knocking at the back door—*knock-knock*!

The woman hurries to the front door, and the farmer goes to the back door.

The snowplow man is at the front door. "My snowplow got stuck in the snow," he says. So he comes in to wait till the other snowplows come.

At the back door there are more people who got stuck in the snow.

"Come in, come in," and "Welcome, welcome," say the woman and the farmer.

All night long, people come knocking at the door.

Now there are eighty-four grown-ups, seventeen children, seven babies, six dogs, a cat, a parakeet, a canary, and a little pet skunk in the little old farmhouse.

Outside, it is snowing and snowing and the wind is blowing.

Inside, the babies are yowling, the dogs are yapping, the chicks are chirping, the mothers are scolding.

"It's a shame," says the woman. "It's a shame. All these people and no party. If only there were a crust or a crumb of cake or bread in the house, or a bit of music."

But listen!

Someone is knocking at the door. It is a very special knock—

knock-knock
knock-knock-knock
knock-knock
knock-knock-knock.

The woman hurries to open the door.

It is the K-M man, the man from the K-M Bakery. His delivery truck is stuck in the snow right in front of the door.

"Come in, come in," says the woman, "and welcome!"

The K-M man comes in, and he looks around at all the people there, and he says, "You look like mighty hungry people to me."

And the woman says, "There's not a crust nor a crumb of bread or cake in the house, but you're welcome to come in out of the wind and the snow."

"Who will help me?" says the K-M man. "Who will help me un-load my truck?" Then he chooses some of the children and some of the grown-up men.

What a parade!

First come the trays full of rolls—crunchy, crusty rolls, brown and shiny; soft, fluffy rolls, white and powdery; poppy seed rolls, sesame seed rolls, little rolls braided like ribbons; smooth, round rolls, shaped like a baby's bottom.

Then come trays of cinnamon buns. The cinnamon makes the air smell like perfume.

Now comes a special parade of pies—lemon meringue pies, cherry pies, coconut custard pies, chocolate cream pies.

Now come the cupcakes—chocolate, vanilla—with pink icing, white icing, rich chocolate icing.

The woman jumps up and down and claps her hands. "It's a party," she says. "It's a party sure enough."

"Ha," says the K-M man. "If it's a party, I'd better bring in my special-order chocolate fudge party cake."

So he brings it in, and the woman puts candles all around it, and somebody makes party hats out of newspapers, and they all eat to their hearts' content.

Then the accordion player plays her accordion, and she plays such lively tunes that no one can sit still. They all stamp their feet to the music. Even the babies wave their fat little hands and feet in time to the music.

Now the accordion player plays a waltz tune, and the farmer grabs the woman around the waist and waltzes with her till they are both out of breath (which doesn't take very long), and everybody claps hands, and they all begin to dance too.

The accordion player plays and plays. She plays "Turkey in the Hay, Turkey in the Straw," and she plays "Pop Goes the Weasel," and she plays "I Put My Left Foot In." Oh, she knows a hundred tunes, and she plays them all!

It's a party, all right. There is feasting and dancing and merry-making. There are high jinks and low jinks. It's a fine party, I can tell you.

The party lasts until noontime—when the snow stops snowing and the wind stops blowing, and the snowplows come through and clear the road.

Everyone says goodbye and thank you to the woman and the man, and they all say it is the best party they have ever been to.

The woman is so content and so happy and so tired and so sleepy that she rests her head on the table next to a coconut custard pie and falls fast asleep...

...and dreams about the party all over again.